Hilary McKay

The Flying Feeling

Hilary McKay

The Flying Feeling

Hodder
Children's
Books

A division of Hodder Headline Limited

First published in Great Britain in 2005
by Hodder Children's Books

The right of Hilary McKay to be identified as the Author
of the Work has been asserted by her in accordance with the
Copyright, Designs and Patents Act 1988.

2 4 6 8 10 9 7 5 3 1

A Catalogue record for this book is available
from the British Library

ISBN 0 340 89426 1

Typeset in Bembo by Avon DataSet Ltd,
Bidford-on-Avon, Warwickshire

Printed and bound in Great Britain by
Clays Ltd, St Ives plc, Bungay, Suffolk

Our grateful thanks to Avon DataSet Ltd, Saxon,
Norske Skog Union, Enso Publication Papers,
Paper Management Services and Clays Ltd

The paper and board used in this paperback by Hodder Children's
Books are natural recyclable products made from wood grown
in sustainable forests. The manufacturing processes conform
to the environmental regulations of the country of origin.

Hodder Children's Books
a division of Hodder Headline Ltd
338 Euston Road
London NW1 3BH

To Ms Damms' Class 8P, at St. Paul's Way Community School. Because they invented Ghost Club!

THE FLYING FEELING

Today I fell asleep in class. School had hardly begun (it was Literacy Hour). Miss Farley, my class teacher, touched me on my shoulder to wake me up.

'NO NO,' I shouted very loudly, and fell on the floor and crawled under the table to escape.

Then I realised where I was, so I came out and sat down again as quietly as I could. I hoped that if I was quick and quiet enough Miss Farley almost would not notice I had done anything unusual. But she did.

Miss Farley said, 'Rose, is there anything wrong? Here at school? Or at home, perhaps?'

I could tell by the way she looked at me that she had not forgotten about yesterday.

WHY I FELL ASLEEP IN CLASS
A LONG THOUGHT
By Rose Casson
Class 4

Miss Farley has a big cheek asking me if there is anything wrong like that. In front of everyone. How would she like it if I did it to her? On one of those days when she comes in with little eyes and no lipstick and snaps, 'Right Class 4, we will separate these groups of tables into lines, since you cannot seem to behave as you are! Rose Casson, what is so interesting out of that window?' (Sky) 'Also, Rose, since when have tie-dyed T-shirts been school uniform, may I ask? And before you do anything, go to the office and take out that earring and ask them for a recycled envelope to put it in, please.'

On those days, do I ask, 'Miss Farley, is there anything wrong at home? Or at school, perhaps?'

No.

Luckily, she has not noticed my earring today. It is a gold hoop with dangling red crystals on gold links. My sister Saffron gave it to me this morning.

There is a clean patch on the carpet in the reading corner where one of the carpet tiles has been shampooed. So nobody in the class can forget about yesterday either.

Also ghost club has been banned.

GHOST CLUB

On wet lunch breaks at our school you can either go to the hall and play, or stay in your classroom and be as quiet as mice. (If mice are like hamsters they are not very quiet.) That is when we do Ghost Club – Kiran (who used to be my best friend) and me and some of the others.

For Ghost Club we turn off the lights and pull down the blinds as far as they will go and sit in a circle on the floor, on the carpet tiles in the reading corner. Then we very, very quietly, very quietly, really quietly take turns to tell ghost stories.

Yesterday was a rainy day, and so we did

ghost club. First Molly told us about her grandad whose false teeth slid out when he fell asleep watching football.

'I don't think that sounds very scary,' I said.

'Yes, well, OK it is only slightly scary,' agreed Molly, 'but admit it is totally gross!'

I admitted this at once, and then I told about the strange scratchy noises in our house at night which cannot be my sister Caddy's escaped hamsters because they would have died ages ago. According to the Hamster Book.

Everyone at ghost club said their houses made strange noises at night too, which their mothers told them were caused by Central Heating. I explained that we did not have Central Heating.

Kiran hummed like she was bored and picked at a carpet tile and said, 'All houses creak a bit and you can get false tooth glue to keep them in, they advertise it on daytime TV when they know old people are watching. You know my cousin? No, carry on talking about central heating! Maybe I shouldn't tell you!'

So of course we made her tell us.

Kiran's stories are the worst because they are true. They are all about people in her family.

I used to think, Thank goodness I am not related to Kiran. If I was related to Kiran I would not feel safe. Terrible things happen all the time to that family.

'Which cousin?' we asked Kiran, because her family (as well as being unsafe) is enormous.

'My cousin who doesn't go to this school, with the pink jacket,' Kiran told us. 'You know the one?'

'No,' we said.

'Well, you know my auntie who came on visitors' day who had to have all the windows opened very quickly?'

'Yes,' we said.

'That's her mother,' said Kiran. 'She bought my cousin the pink jacket, from the market stall next to the mobile ear-piercing van. And anyway, you know that place by the park near Rose's house where no one is allowed to go?'

'No,' we said.

'Yes you do, it is all fenced in and a notice says DANGER HIGH VOLTAGE.'

'It is an electricity substation,' said Molly, who always knows stuff like that because she goes on Intelligent Quality Time walks with her mother. (I don't.)

'Well,' continued Kiran very quickly, before Molly could start telling us about substations, 'my cousin with the pink jacket was walking past that place and it was winter and it was nearly dark and you know how if you hold your hand up very close to your face and it is nearly dark, all the fingers look thick and black and not real?'

We said no, and then we tried it with our own hands sitting in the nearly-darkness of the reading corner, and then we said, 'Oh yes.'

'A hand like that but much bigger,' said Kiran. She was speaking very quietly indeed now, like she didn't really want us to hear. 'Over her shoulder. And no footprints. No sound of footprints. And not quite touching her. My cousin. And the fingers very thick and dark like a thick dark leather glove. Not smooth leather. Reaching over her shoulder, just at that place by the park where you are not allowed to go. She saw it out of the corner of her eye.'

Nobody said anything.

'She just caught sight of it for a moment. The first time.'

You could hear the clock, and the sound of people being told off in the hall, and you could hear us breathing.

'But she saw it for longer the next time.'

'Did she look around?' whispered Molly.

'Only once.'

'What did she see?'

'She won't tell me.'

'Ki . . . raaan!' we wailed.

'So now she won't wear her pink jacket and my auntie says it is a waste because it was nearly new and she says I can have it and wear it with a scarf. Because they won't wash off; they are burnt on.'

'*WHAT* ARE BURNT ON?' shouted several people.

'The finger marks,' said Kiran, sounding very surprised that we did not know. 'The thick burnt brown finger marks on the shoulder of the jacket.'

We didn't say anything.

'I'm not having that revolting jacket,' said Kiran.

Still nobody said anything. We were thinking. We knew the place by the park where you are not allowed to go. We knew Kiran's auntie who bought the jacket, and we knew the market stall it came from. We even knew the mobile ear-piercing van; my sister Saffron had her nose pierced there. When I thought about it, I thought I even knew Kiran's cousin who doesn't go to this school. And I knew, exactly as if I had seen them, what the thick dark finger marks looked like scorched on to the shoulder of that pink jacket.

Someone grabbed my shoulder very hard and shouted, 'ROSE'S TURN!'

I jumped so badly I felt sick and dizzy and I shouted, 'Not me!' without even meaning to shout, but I don't think it sounded very loud. Everyone was laughing so much.

Kiran said, 'I am sorry, Rose, I am sorry, Rose, I am sorry, Rose!' but I will never forgive her.

If I had a choice between dying and wetting myself in class, I would choose dying.

HAMSTERS

These are the people who live at my house:

1. Me.
2. Mummy, who is called Eve. She is an artist. She does her art in a shed at the bottom of the garden. It is not true that Mummy calls everyone darling to save her bothering to remember names.
3. Indigo, who is my brother and is five years older than me. Indigo is very tall and thin. With his eyes closed he looks dead. He always has, but no one has ever got used to it. This is bad luck for Indigo. It means that ever since he was a baby, frightened people

have been shaking him awake to make sure he is still alive. Over the years Indigo has grown more and more difficult to wake up.

4. Saffron. She is really my cousin, but she is my adopted sister too. She is nearly fifteen and she is very pretty (like Caddy) and very clever (like Indigo). When Saffron found out about yesterday at ghost club she said, 'One way of getting the carpet cleaned, Rosy Pose!'

Saffron is ruthless.

These are the people who do not live at my house:

1. Daddy. He lives in London where he has a studio, because he is an artist too. (He says.)

2. My grown-up sister Caddy who is at university. Before she went to university she kept more guinea pigs and hamsters than most people would want to own. She kept them all over the place. There are still some

guinea pigs left in a hutch in the garden, but the hamsters are all gone.

But where have they gone?

Yesterday evening when my sister Saffron was doing her homework and my brother Indigo was lying on the floor listening to terrible music with his headphones on, I told Mummy what happened at school. She was making an illuminated manuscript because she is having a display of illuminated manuscripts in the library. Poems in old-fashioned writing with little pictures around the capital letters and decorated edges. On this poem she was drawing singing birds, all different bright colours among the leaves.

'I know darling Bill would say it is Not Exactly Art,' she said (Darling Bill is Daddy). 'But it is fun and they sell amazingly well and the suspension on my car has more or less gone completely. These days it is more like sledging along on your bottom than real driving so I will have to get it fixed and goodness knows what it will cost. Do you like the poem, Rosy Pose? It is tenth-century Irish. Translated. Caddy used to have accidents at school so often that I put dry knickers in every morning with her packed lunch. Until she started school dinners.'

Then there was a big bang and all the lights went out.

'Goodness,' said Mummy after a minute or two. 'Or is it just one bulb?'

Indigo continued to lie on the floor with his eyes shut droning away to his terrible music, because he was running on batteries.

'No, it isn't just one bulb,' said Mummy, futilely flicking switches. 'It is all over the house.' Then she accidentally trod on Indigo and he unplugged himself and said, 'Candles.'

'I know,' said Mummy. 'But unfortunately not. I threw them all away after I had a terrible dream about Rose accidentally setting the house on fire. In case it was a warning. And I took that big cinnamon-scented one in to college to relax my Young Offenders only last week . . .' (Mummy teaches Art to Young Offenders so that they can do their vandalising with style and confidence, Daddy says.) '. . . and it is still there.'

'Did it relax them?' enquired Indigo.

'Yes and no,' said Mummy. 'I had to blow it out because a very naughty little boy used it to light up a . . . Well, never mind! He was surprised that I recognised the smell. (Poor darling.) I wonder if the power is off in the shed?'

Indigo said he would go and see and he went outside and did, and it wasn't because the shed was properly wired by an intelligent hippy who lived in a tent and who (briefly) fell in love with Caddy and then Mummy. He unblocked the sink too. But soon after that he went to Tangier in an old bus. His name was Derek, and he would have taken Mummy to Tangier with him, and me and Indy and Saffron too, and Caddy could have visited for holidays. There was plenty of room in the bus. But we didn't go. Because Mummy said, 'What about darling Bill?'

And Derek said there wasn't that much room in the bus.

What has this got to do with why I fell asleep in class?

Everything.

But what has it go to do with hamsters?

We didn't find out till morning.

Mummy said, 'Oh good, that solves everything!' when she heard there was still power in the shed.

Mummy would be perfectly happy to live in the shed.

SAFFRON, SARAH,
ORLANDO BLOOM
AND THE DARK

Indigo found two torches, one for him and one for me, and he gave me the brightest because you do not need much light to listen to music. It is best in the dark. Mummy went out to do her illuminated manuscript in the shed and Saffron came groping and grumbling down the stairs because of her homework.

'This is so not a good time to be plunged into darkness,' she said, flapping her hands about. 'Where has everyone gone?'

'I am here,' I said, shining my torch in my face so she screamed. 'And Mummy is in the shed where it is still light and Indy is on the floor beside me. It is a power cut.'

'If there is still light in the shed then it is not a power cut,' said Saffron. 'It is an Electrical Problem in this house. Right in the middle of my maths homework and I have just varnished my nails and they are still sticky.' (That was why she was flapping her hands so much. To dry her nails.) 'It is not fair. I wanted to get 100% because we have a new student teacher for maths until the end of term and he looks exactly like Orlando Bloom only without the bow and arrows and gold teeth and sandals and he will be marking it.'

She said this while groping her way very carefully to the phone so as not to ruin her nails. 'I am ringing up Sarah,' said Saffron. (Sarah is her best friend.) 'I bet they haven't got a power cut.'

So she did and they hadn't.

Then Saffron and Sarah had a huge conversation in the dark (at our end) about nail varnish and maths homework and gold teeth and it ended up an argument.

'Why do best friends argue so much more than ordinary friends?' I asked Indigo, whose batteries were going flat.

'Because they listen to each other so much more than ordinary friends,' said Indigo.

Sarah's house is very close to ours, just down the road, past the park. After the telephone argument Saffron went to Sarah's house to prove she was right. She took her maths homework with her, and her nail varnish, and her night things, because Sarah's mother said she and Sarah's father were going out and would not be back till late and if Saffron would like to stay the night, that would be perfect. I like Sarah's mother. She always makes you feel like just the person she was hoping to see. Especially if you go round at mealtimes when she says, 'Wonderful! I have cooked far too much for just us,' and gets out extra bread and salad and lets me hunt in the freezer for pudding. It is easy to stay the night at Sarah's house because Sarah has an enormous bedroom with two beds and a hammock in it. Ever since I first saw it I have wanted to sleep in Sarah's hammock.

When Saffron had gone the house felt very lonely indeed. And dark. Especially when Indigo took the batteries out of his torch and put them in his cd player. Then we only had one working torch left.

'What can you do when it is as dark as this?' I asked Indigo.

'Go to bed,' said Indigo.

After a while I did go to bed. Mummy wasn't coming back into the house, I knew. She would finish her manuscript and then she would lie down on the old pink sofa she keeps in her shed, and then she would accidentally fall asleep, and she would still be there in the morning.

I hate it when Mummy goes to sleep in the shed by accident.

Especially when there is no one in the house except Indigo and me.

And the lights don't work.

And it has been a horrible day.

THE LIGHTNING
IN THE SHED
(PART ONE)

When I was in bed I tried very hard not to think about what happened to me in the reading corner, and about Kiran's cousin's pink jacket, and the dark unreal hand over her shoulder and the way she looked back once and would not tell Kiran what she saw.

And how Kiran's quiet voice sounded when she said, 'I don't want that revolting jacket.'

It was very hard not to think of these things. So I concentrated on what I could hear and there were sounds in the walls. Scrabbly sounds like giant spiders would make. I got up and made Indigo turn his music off and come and listen.

'Nope,' said Indigo. 'I can't hear a thing. Not a single spider. Not a leg. Go back to bed, Rosy Pose.'

I went back to bed and to stop myself listening I felt my neck to see if I had any lumps growing there.

Kiran's cousin once had a lump on her neck. Not the cousin with the jacket, another cousin with very long hair. She got the lump when she went on holiday to a very hot place, where she bought Kiran a bracelet made of shells and silver beads and string, which Kiran used to wear to school until the string got dirty. And then she washed it and all the silver came off the beads and they were plastic underneath.

At first Kiran's cousin's lump was little, but it got bigger. It grew. I know exactly where. On the back of her neck just where her head joins on. I have a little mole in the same place. And the lump grew and it itched but Kiran's cousin's hair covered it up and she did not tell anyone, and it grew bigger. And then one day when Kiran's cousin was brushing her hair she banged the lump with her hairbrush and it opened. And Kiran's cousin screamed and screamed and out poured spiders. Dozens and dozens of black spiders.

I got out of bed again and went to Indigo's room and asked Indigo to check my neck for spider lumps.

He checked very carefully and patiently and he said there were none at all, and he said the sounds I could hear were probably hamsters in the walls.

'Maybe it is Joseph,' said Indigo. Joseph was a hamster with fur which was all different colours (which was why he was called Joseph). 'Or Blossom,' said Indigo. (Blossom had a white flower-shaped mark in the middle of her back.)

But Joseph and Blossom escaped long ago, and hamsters do not live very long. They would have died by now. We have a hamster book which explains this. And if they had not died they would have killed each other because that is what hamsters do. They fight to the death. The hamster book says that too. So.

I told Indigo this and he said, 'But Joseph and Blossom have not read the hamster book. So you never know. Go back to bed, Rosy Pose.'

I went back to bed, and I thought about Joseph and Blossom. Somewhere Joseph and Blossom are dead in this house.

This was not a nice thought, and as soon as I had thought it I wished I hadn't. I especially wished I had not thought the word HOUSE.

It reminded me of what happened to another of Kiran's aunties.

She used to have a dream. It was a dream of a house that she had never seen. A lovely house, in the country. She dreamed of it so often, and for so many years, that it felt like her own house, even though she had never been there in real life.

And then one day when she was driving in the country she saw it. Her house. Exactly like her dreams. And it was for sale.

So Kiran's aunt stopped the car and she jumped out and she ran to the gate, and across the sunny garden and up to the house, just as she had run so many times in her dreams. And she knocked at the door.

A man opened it and he stared at Kiran's aunt.

'Oh please,' she said. 'Please tell me. Is this house really for sale?'

'Yes,' he said, staring and staring and shaking too. Shaking and grey. 'Yes it is. But you wouldn't want to buy it.'

'Why not?' asked Kiran's aunt.

'It's haunted,' said the man.

'Haunted?' said Kiran's aunt, and she laughed.

'Don't laugh,' said the man.

But Kiran's aunt still laughed and she said, 'Is it haunted often?'

'Yes,' said the man. 'Often. Often. As it has been for years. You should know. YOU ARE THE GHOST THAT HAUNTS THIS HOUSE!'

Then the man fell down dead on the doorstep.

Then Kiran's poor aunt ran screaming away across the sunny garden and out into the road and straight under a lorry that was coming from the quarry round the corner.

And it killed her.

Indigo was very grumpy when I woke him up to tell him this story and he said, 'If the man at the door died and Kiran's aunt died then how does Kiran know anything about it?'

'Of course she knows about it,' I said. 'It was her aunt. Indigo, do you think this house is haunted?'

'No,' said Indigo. 'This is the least haunted house in the world. There's always someone awake in it. Or being shaken awake. You are quite safe. And Saffy is safe at Sarah's. And Mum is safe in the shed. So go back to bed, Rosy Pose.'

THE LIGHTNING
IN THE SHED
(PART TWO)

But is Mummy safe in the shed?

There is no lock on the door of the shed.

Indigo has never been so hard to wake up, but I managed it in the end and at last he sat up all sleepy and groaning and he said, 'Now what?'

I said, 'What if someone comes in the night and murders Mummy in the shed?'

Indigo was not cross but he was not very interested either. He said, 'What would be the point?'

'Murderers do not need a point,' I said. 'They do it for fun.'

'I don't think it would be much fun murdering Mum in the shed,' said Indigo.

'But you are not a murderer,' I pointed out.

Indigo made a growling noise and pulled his quilt over his head, but then he pulled it off again and said, 'I do not think Mum is in any danger of being murdered in the shed. I think she has less chance of being murdered in the shed than she has of being struck by lightning.'

This cheered me up at once because although I have always been slightly worried about Mum being murdered in the shed I have never been the slightest bit afraid of her being struck by lightning.

'If you are really scared,' said Indigo (who had got his eyes open now) 'I will take you to the shed to check she has not been murdered. Or struck by lightning. But,' (he pulled back the curtain beside his bed and looked out) 'it is raining.'

'Is it thundering?' I asked.

'No,' said Indigo. 'It is just plain raining. It is not thundering or lightning.'

'Then we will leave her where she is,' I said.

'Oh good,' said Indigo.

Then he put his headphones on.

Next he put his head under his pillow.

After that he pulled his quilt over his pillow.

From underneath he said, 'Don't wake me up again, please, Rosy Pose.'

THE LIGHTNING
IN THE SHED
(PART THREE)

I went back to bed and thought about things.

Nothing good.

And I must have fallen asleep.

I know I must have fallen asleep, because I remember dreaming. I dreamed that lorries were driving over the roof of the house, dragging huge chains behind them like snail trails. I could still hear them when I woke up. It sounded like thunder.

It was thunder. And the rain was much harder now than it had been before. It was hitting my bedroom window with a rattle like stones, but

I think it was the lightning that woke me up.

The lightning was so bright I could see the flashes with my eyes shut.

And the power was off.

And Saffy was at Sarah's house.

And Indigo would not wake up.

And Mummy was asleep in the shed.

Afterwards, Saffy gave me this earring that Miss Farley has not noticed yet, as a reward for my bravery in going to rescue Mummy from the lightning in the shed.

Sometimes when people get rewards for bravery they say, 'Oh, I was not really brave. I do not deserve a reward. Anyone would have done the same.'

But it was not like that for me. I was very brave. I think I did deserve a reward. Because it was very scary going downstairs in the dark to rescue Mummy, and as I crossed the living-room floor my bare toe touched something warm and limp and furry and I saw by a flash of lightning that it was Joseph's ghost.

I rushed across the room to the kitchen, crossed the kitchen and opened the back door. When I saw exactly what it was like outside I nearly didn't go any further.

But I did.

When I went outside I was wearing:

1. My pyjamas.

2. Indigo's denim jacket.

3. Saffy's old trainers.

I found the jacket and the trainers in the kitchen by lightning because the power was still off.

There was no light on in the shed. I would have to wake Mummy up before I could rescue her.

Outside, the rain was so cold it hurt and the wind had gone mad and was blowing in four directions at once, tearing at Indigo's jacket as if it knew he had not said I could wear it. But worst of all were Saffy's trainers. They were so much too big that although I wanted more than anything to run, I had to walk quite slowly. Behind me the kitchen door banged shut. I wrapped my arms tightly around myself and shuffled along the garden path.

Mummy was not in the shed.

The shed was just the same, with the canvases toppling against the walls, and jamjars full of paintbrushes, and the little yellow table with the kettle and the jar of instant coffee and the bag of guinea pig food. The pink sofa was there, with the old quilt Mummy brought back from India, but Mummy was not asleep on it.

I thought of murderers at once and I shut my eyes very tightly in case there was blood.

Then I opened them, and there was no blood.

There is nowhere in the shed that anyone could hide except under the sofa, but there was no one under the sofa. I know because I checked.

Anyone who checks under a sofa in a shed in a thunderstorm in the middle of the night for either:

1. Their mother's body.

or

2. Whoever got their mother.

Is very brave indeed.

That was me.

After I had checked under the sofa, I started looking round the shed for clues. It seemed to me that if Mummy was not in the shed, then someone or something must have got her. I could not rescue her if I did not know who, or what. That was why I looked for clues.

The only thing different or new was the illuminated poem on the table. It was finished now; the colours, red and green and blue and gold, all very bright and clear. Mummy says when she does her decorated poems, 'The trick is not to make them look like wall paper.'

This one did not look like wall paper, but I did not look at it properly because I was having another horrible thought. I was thinking whoever (or whatever) got Mummy might now come back for me.

In nearly no time at all I kicked off Saffy's trainers and got out of that shed and back to the house.

I got back to the house, and that was the worst problem yet.

The door was shut. I had heard it shut as I went to the shed, but I was concentrating so much on rescuing Mummy from the lightning and not falling over in Saffron's trainers that I had not really noticed. The door has the sort of lock that locks itself when it shuts, and this had happened and I was locked out.

Now the lightning was flashing so often that it was on more than it was off, and the thunder and the rain were stronger than ever, and I was locked out and I rang the doorbell and rang the doorbell and rang the doorbell and Indigo did not come.

And then I remembered that it was an electric doorbell and so of course it was not working.

How wrong I was to think that I was safe because all the terrible things happened to Kiran's family.

THE LIGHTNING
IN THE SHED
(PART FOUR)

I had not stopped being brave yet (although I would have liked to). I had to decide what to do, and these were my choices:

1. Go back to the shed and wait for whatever got Mummy to come and get me.

2. Sit on the doorstep and wait for whatever got Mummy to come and get me OR to be struck by lightning.

3. Run for help to Sarah's house.

The trouble with running for help to Sarah's house was that on the way I risked being got by whatever got Mummy AND being struck by lightning AND as well the way to Sarah's house is past the park and the place where it says DANGER HIGH VOLTAGE and you are not allowed to go. And I had not forgotten that this was the place where the hand reached out. The hand that scorched the pink jacket of Kiran's cousin who does not go to our school.

But I could not bear to go back to the shed and it was terrible on the doorstep and I thought I might survive the journey to Sarah's house because I can run very fast (only not in Saffron's trainers).

It takes about three minutes to walk to Sarah's house, but if you run in bare feet in a thunder storm in the middle of the night with you-don't-know-what behind you and even worse in front, it takes about a minute and a half. This is what I did, and I was past the place where it said DANGER HIGH VOLTAGE before I had hardly taken a breath.

And then I could not help it. I looked back.

There is a cherry tree just behind the DANGER HIGH VOLTAGE place, and its branches hang low over the pavement and one has been trimmed so that it looks just like a hand. A dark hand with bent fingers in a thick leather glove.

But it was only a branch of cherry tree.

Of course I shall not tell that to the Horror Club (which I intend to start as soon as possible).

I shall say, 'How lucky it is that I was wearing Indigo's jacket which is blacky-brown and does not show scorch marks.'

And I shall not tell them that as soon as I knew Kiran's cousin's terrible hand was a branch of cherry tree I knew something else too.

I knew where Mummy was.

In bed.

Humans cannot fly, but they can get the flying feeling. All they need to do is go out at night into a wild storm where the thunder roars like applause and the lightning throws itself in daggers of light at your bare feet and you suddenly find you are not afraid.

Saffron and Sarah were not asleep. They were watching the storm from Sarah's bedroom window and they saw me at once so that before I could reach the front door of the house it was open and Saffron and Sarah and Sarah's parents too were all pulling me inside.

And I was quite right, Mummy was in bed. Sarah's mother rang up and found out.

Then everyone had hot chocolate except Sarah's father (who had whisky) and I had a hot bath too. And afterwards Saffron and Sarah put me to bed in the hammock. You have to be put to bed in a hammock. It is impossible to do it yourself, but it is lovely when you are in.

Sarah's mother turned the light off and she said, 'You are my favourite guest, Rose, but it is after three o'clock in the morning. I will make you pancakes for breakfast if you go to sleep this second WITH NO MORE FUSS.'

So I did.

WHY I FELL ASLEEP IN CLASS
By Rose Casson
Class 4
Part Two

'Tired people cannot learn,' said Miss Farley, dumping a handful of marker pens into a full mug of coffee and trying to look like she had meant to do it.

But that is not true. Tired people can learn (and learning is tiring). I am very tired and I have learned a lot since yesterday.

Things I have Learned Since Yesterday

1. Hamsters

Hamsters do not always do what it says in the hamster book. Because after Joseph and Blossom escaped they made friends and lived wild in the house and had a lot of children. And they lived for twice as long as they were meant to do, and Joseph chewed through the television cable and caused a power cut which temporarily stunned him until I touched him with my foot and woke him up. It was not his ghost after all, it was the real Joseph. Indigo found him in the living-room this morning, asleep under a sofa cushion. As soon as Joseph saw Indigo he ran off. Indigo said he looked slightly guilty but otherwise perfectly well.

2. Kiran's family

Maybe it is true that Kiran's family have all the terrible things happen to them. But maybe not. Because at breakfast time while we were eating pancakes I told everyone the things Kiran had told us at ghost club. And Sarah's mother said, 'Oh, the spider story! I had forgotten the spider story!'

'Do you know Kiran's cousin?' I asked, very surprised.

'No,' said Sarah's mother, 'but I know that story! I heard it when I was a little girl with long hair. I was told it by my brother who had a friend who had a sister who still had the scar to prove it!'

She knew the one about Kiran's aunty and the dream house too. 'Those stories have been old for a very long time,' she said. 'I am glad to hear they are still being told. Your friend sounds an excellent story-teller!'

So maybe Kiran's family do not have all the bad luck in the world. Maybe they just have Kiran.

3. The Flying Feeling

The worst thing about coming to school this morning was the clean patch on the carpet tiles in the reading corner. I did not know how I could bear to look at the reading corner ever again. I knew that everyone else was looking at it. And remembering what happened. And I knew they always would. I know Class 4. They never forget anything.

I thought, If I don't look everyone will know why I am not looking. And I thought, If I do look everyone will know that I am trying to pretend I don't care.

All the same I could not help looking to see how much the clean patch showed.

It showed a lot.

Everyone looked at me looking at it and they saw that I saw that it showed a lot.

Suddenly I thought of Saffron, and without realising it, I said out loud what Saffron said the night before. I said, 'I suppose it was one way of getting the carpet cleaned.'

If you can make people laugh, if you can make them *really* laugh, then they cannot laugh at you.

Also you get the Flying Feeling.

Appendices

Appendices are the extra bits at the end of a story which people might want to know. Or not. It depends whether the story is any good.

Appendix I
Why I only wear one earring

The reason I only wear one earring is that when Saffron and Sarah took me to get my ears pierced, I did not know what it would be like. They said it would not hurt much, and they were telling the truth. It did not hurt much.

'You will hear a sort of pop,' they said, 'and then it will be done.'

That was true too, I did hear a sort of pop, and then it was done, and I had a right ear that could wear earrings. But I did not like that pop. It felt like being slightly but definitely shot.

Nothing Saffron and Sarah could say could make me let them shoot me twice.

That is why I only wear one earring.

One is enough.

Appendix II
Mummy's poem

I cannot tell anyone what this poem means. I do not know. I cannot explain why I like it either. But I do.

> Round the tree of Life the flowers
> Are ranged, abundant, even;
> Its crest on every side spread out
> On the fields and plains of Heaven
>
> Glorious flocks of singing birds
> Celebrate their truth,
> Green abounding branches bear
> Choicest leaves and fruit.
>
> The lovely flocks maintain their song
> In the changeless weather.
> A hundred feathers for every bird
> A hundred songs for every feather.

Appendix III
Miss Farley

Miss Farley laughed as much as everyone else when I said, 'One way of getting the carpet cleaned.' Also she stopped trying to pretend she had meant to put her pens in her cold coffee. She said, 'Good grief, look what I have done! I must be totally losing it at last. Rose, do you think you could go and get me a handful of paper towels, and while you are out pop into the office and ask for a recycled envelope to put that . . . Oh, never mind. I will try and only see your left ear, just for today.'

At breaktime we noticed she put her lipstick on.

Also at breaktime I told Kiran about the Lightning in the Shed. Kiran said I was ten million times braver than anyone she'd ever known including her big brother's friend's big brother.

'Never heard of him,' I said.

'Yes, you have,' said Kiran. 'He is the one

who missed firework night because he ran three times the wrong way round a church at Hallowe'en in order to find out what would happen.'

'What did happen?' I asked.

'Oh well,' said Kiran, 'a black thing came out of one of the graves and said, "I've been waiting a long time for a fool to come and take my place." And it rushed towards him and he fell over and cracked his head on a tombstone and missed firework night . . .'

I have decided that Kiran just cannot help it.

It is nice being best friends again, and now there is nothing wrong anywhere, at home or at school.

Another Hodder Children's book by Hilary McKay

SAFFY'S ANGEL
Winner of the Whitbread Children's Book Award

Introducing the Casson family:

Caddy is the eldest. She's on her ninety-sixth driving lesson and she's mad about her gorgeous instructor. Indigo is an outrageous cook and survives as the only boy in a pack of girls. Rose, the youngest, is a whiz at art, and knows just how to manage her parents. And outsider Saffy – she's simply in search of her angel.

A hilarious, touching novel by a multi award-winning author.

Indigo's Star

Indigo's returning to school after a bout of glandular fever and is dreading it. Rose is worrying about Indigo – and her new glasses. Saffy is busy dictating Rose's homework answers, while Caddy agonises over ways to dump her current boyfriend. And their mother, Eve, is busy trying to dry her painting with a hairdryer.

But Tom has joined Indigo's class. And that will make all the difference . . .

'*As funny and compelling as her Whitbread-winning Saffy's Angel . . . Definitely a book to curl up with and enjoy in one single sitting.*' Lesley Agnew, The Bookseller.